# Pete the Kitty

## AND THE GROOVY PLAYDATE

Kimberly and James Dean

HARPER

An Imprint of HarperCollinsPublishers

Pete the Kitty and the Groovy Playdate
Text copyright © 2018 by Kimberly and James Dean
Illustrations copyright © 2018 by James Dean
Pete the Cat is a registered trademark of Pete the Cat, LLC.
All rights reserved. Printed in the United States of America.

www.harpercollinschildrens.com

ISBN 978-0-06-267540-8 [trade bdg.]
ISBN 978-0-06-267541-5 [lib. bdg.]

The artist used pen and ink with watercolor and acrylic paint on 300lb press paper
to create the illustrations for this book.
Typography by Jeanne L. Hogle
18 19 20 21 22   PC   10 9 8 7 6 5 4 3 2 1
❖
First Edition

2 Corinthians 9:7
—J.D. & K.D.

Pete the Kitty jumps out of bed!
"I cannot wait! Grumpy Toad and
I have a GROOVY playdate."

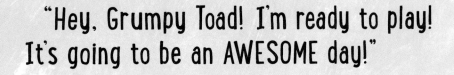

"Hey, Grumpy Toad! I'm ready to play!
It's going to be an AWESOME day!"

Pete wants to play with Grumpy Toad's cool blue truck!

ZOOM
ZOOM
VROOM
all around the room!

But Grumpy Toad
starts to whine.

"That truck is
MINE! MINE! MINE!"

Pete the Kitty says, "No worries! That's okay!
I'll find something else to play."

Pete finds some blocks.
"Let's build a city!" says Pete the Kitty.

But Grumpy Toad
starts to whine.

"Those blocks are
MINE! MINE! MINE!"

Pete the Kitty says, "No
worries! That's okay! I'll find
something else to play."

Pete sees a superhero cape.

"Far out!"

# "HAVE NO FEAR! SUPER KITTY IS HERE!"

But Grumpy Toad starts to whine.

Grumpy Toad has all the toys and Pete has none.

This playdate is just not fun!

Pete is sad. Pete is blue.
He thinks about what to do.

"Grumpy Toad, wouldn't it be better
if we were playing together?"

Grumpy Toad says, "My pile of toys has grown. But it's no fun playing alone."

Grumpy Toad thinks of all the fun
he and Pete have together.

"Yes! Sharing would make this playdate so much better!"

# Grumpy Toad shares his truck with Pete!

"You push me and I'll push you . . .

ZOOM
ZOOM
VROOM

all around the room!"

# Grumpy Toad shares his blocks!

"Here are the blocks, Pete the Kitty,
for you and me to build a city!"

Grumpy Toad shares his cape!

Okay! Time for superheroes to save the day!

"Have no fear! Wonder Toad and Super Kitty are here!"

Grumpy Toad shares
ALL his toys with Pete.

They play and
play . . .

and play!

What a GROOVY, awesome day!

"Thank you, Grumpy Toad, for sharing
your cape, your truck, and your blocks!"